BIG ASS ALIENS
BOOK 1

T. Aaron Cisco

ISBN: 9781071124413

Dedicated to Cat, my incredible sister.

NORTH LOOP

"Thanks for coming last tonight."

"No problem. I'm always up for free drinks."

"It's nice to have someone who can talk about something other than their latest RPG character twists."

"Yeah those guys are pretty weird."

"I know you said you had to work tonight, but would you want to maybe grab a nightcap at my place after?"

"Your…place?"

"Yeah, my place. Is that…cool?"

"Uh Cory, we should talk."

"Aw man, I came on too strong, didn't I? I'm not the smoothest guy. I just thought we had a nice time and--"

"You're a really nice guy—"

"--And we spent like, two hours making out and--."

"--but I don't date Black guys."

"—then we...wait, what?"

"I don't date Black guys. It's nothing personal. I'm just not attracted to Black guys. It's not a race thing."

"How is it not a race thing?"

"Because it's not racism, it's just a preference."

"That's what racism is…a preference…for one race over others. I mean, it's obviously not going to work, but what I'm trying to figure out is…last night was our fourth date."

"So what, you think because we went out a couple times, you own me? Now who's the racist?"

"That's not what that...you know what, forget it. Just one thing though. And I'm sure I'm going to regret asking, but I have to know. If you don't date people like me, then why'd you agree to go out the first time...and the second...and third...and...?"

"I read this blog about how like, most white people only date other white people. And like, I don't want to be 'other' white people. They're so closed minded."

"Jesus Christ..."

"I realized that like, all of my friends and family? Everybody's white. I don't want them thinking I'm a racist. I'm an activist, y'know. I'm an ally. And I don't care what people think, but I've got to make sure that people don't see me the wrong way."

"Okay, just so I've got this straight...you went out with someone you weren't interested in- solely because of their skin color- to prove, hypothetically, that you don't judge people based on their skin color?"

"I'm not color blind. I just respect my place in your world. You made it out of the hood. You should be proud."

"The hood? We're from the same neighborhood!"

"You know what I mean."

"I shouldn't have asked. Bye."

"But wait.."

I cut off the call and looked out of the window. Just past the fog-shrouded silhouettes of the condominium developments on the other side of the Mississippi river, I glimpsed a shockingly gargantuan, vaguely humanoid shape emerge briefly in the distance. I squinted and leaned forward, but the form quickly vanished behind the thick veil of grey clouds and blowing snow.

I shook my head, exasperated at myself for letting lack of sleep and a hyper-active imagination get the best of me. I checked my watch, certain that I'd killed at least an hour of the morning, but sadly, the face of my comfortably expensive timepiece confirmed that it had indeed only been twenty two minutes.

I set my tablet aside and fired up the chess puzzle app on my desktop. Whenever my day dragged- or I was impossibly annoyed by conversations with racists- losing myself in a few challenging endgame scenarios always made the time fly. I hadn't played against a live, face-to-face, human opponent in almost ten years, but the digital games kept my skills sharp,

Having been bullied endlessly as a child for my bookish nature, awkward stature, and ambivalence towards the latest trends, I found sanctuary within "nerdy" endeavors. I didn't know I wasn't cool. I just liked what I liked.

Between the pages of Michael Crichton, Judy Blume and Edgar Allan Poe I was free from the name-calling and insults. The hours spent watching Star Trek and Doctor Who reruns were hours in which I was safe from the insulting jokes and painful jabs, the rude heckles and brutish shoves, the black eyes and sucker punches.

While the other kids hung around the usual neighborhood spots talking about popstar publicity stunts, I was hanging in my bedroom, reading the linear notes on my records, basking in the auditory brilliance of Leonard Bernstein conducting the New York Philharmonic, or being hypnotized by the astoundingly compelling arrangement of Yusef Lateef's take on The Beatles' Hey Jude.

My awkward social skills were offset by a perspicacious focus on studying. All that time spent acquiring a wide variety of knowledge on an even wider variety of topics got me a nice position with a lucrative company that ironically, was staffed with the kind of people I never would've associated with back in the day. My colleagues respect my position, but they're too busy indulging in mid-sized marketing firm perks to notice anything. They were happy to wear jeans to work and play foosball. They couldn't care less why the well-dressed, black man in the corner office didn't spend his mornings at the coffee stations chatting about predictable movies and cookie-cutter music.

I headed outside for a quick smoke. Even in the midst of a an April storm, the view was gorgeous. Hundreds of Minneapolites who found their morning commute dashed by the seasonably appropriate (but still unexpected) post-Easter onslaught of sleet and snow, showed their unique brand of upper Midwest heartiness by refusing to let the thermometer dictate their sartorial choices. The walking trails and bike paths that coiled in perfect parallel along the riverbanks, were packed with a sea of color and fabrics.

I didn't like thinking about the past. Nostalgia is deadlier than the poisons I'd just been inhaling. We'd been warned about the dangers of tobacco, nicotine, and carcinogens for as long as I can remember, but not once had anyone ever mentioned how focusing too much on the rearview- even when it's right behind you- could be just as detrimental.

I finished my smoke, and headed back upstairs. A clap of thunder tore through the quiet calm of the empty office causing me to jump. Snowfall and thunder are a hellish combination, but for a seasoned veteran of the Twin Cities, I really should have known better.

Chuckling to myself, I sat down and checked a few emails, then reviewed the meeting schedule for the day. The rows of empty white cells on my calendar always made me smile. Aside from a check-in conference call with the a tech vendor, my entire day was clear.

I'd just opened the latest report, and was beginning to update the quarterly analytics when I felt someone watching me. At first, I thought it may have been Hector and his window washing crew, but the weather wasn't right for dangling dozens of stories above the sidewalk.

I resumed reviewing the reports, when I felt it again. This time it wasn't coming from outside the window. The unsettling energy emanated from behind the office door. Even before the second series of rhythmic knocking finished, I knew who it was. And at this time of morning, the person standing on the other side wasn't coming to visit for any business-related matters.

Although I consider myself to be a fastidious, experienced professional who could handle all kinds of surprises, I hated unscheduled visits. Definitely not when the unscheduled visitor was the obtuse pile of microaggressive obliviousness with a bad haircut, currently standing in my doorway.

"Come in!"

"What's up Cory! How you feeling fam?"

To call Weston annoying is like saying the ocean has a few fish. It was an understatement so grossly incomplete, that it rubbed right up against the border of fallacious. Weston was a "wokie-dope," someone who tried way too hard to be seen as progressive as long as it was trendy.

If Weston spent even a tenth of the energy he wasted on trying to be perceived as agreeing with a good cause, on actually doing something towards that good cause, many social and economic woes would be practically eradicated. We'd mildly butted heads numerous times over the years. Every argument was the same. He'd come running into my office because some podcast he'd listened to on the way to work mentioned something "new" like *housing discrimination*, *educational disparities*, or *police brutality*, and he'd be excited to tell me how much he vehemently disagreed with whatever issue was trending online.It wouldn't have been so bad if he actually was learning about these issues, but his behavior was still blatantly oafish.

He didn't get that if you're still objectifying and disrespecting women, it doesn't matter how many tee shirts with the word "Feminist" screen-printed across the front you buy. It doesn't matter how many non-white authors and artists you can name, if you're uncomfortable around non-white people in real life. Nobody cares that you like rap.

Weston wasn't as bad as he could've been. It was better than him being some wild bigot with a popped collar and red baseball cap complaining about the problems of privilege. But that didn't mean his obsession with being seen as the vanguard of inclusion wasn't annoying. And if he wasn't one of the partners, I'd have told him so.

"I'm fine, Weston. How are you?"

"I told you my brother, you can call me Dub-Dub."

If Weston was like most Minnesotans, he'd limit himself to just enough interactions to have plausible deniability if anyone ever accused him of being a racist. He relentlessly tried to connect- not with me, but rather his stereotypical idea of what I should be.

"I'm not calling you that."

"You seem a little off today, What's up with you? Didn't I see you with Caitlyn last night? How's that going?"

"That's not a thing anymore."

"Aw that's too bad, man. She was cute for a white girl."

"Can I help you with something, Weston?"

"Nah I'm good. You know how it is. Can you believe that weather out there, bro? It's like *The Man* can't let us have nothing nice."

"How is 'The Man,' responsible for snowfall?"

"You know that severe weather changes are due to climate change, right?"

"Right. Still not following you."

"All those political moves from the rich white politicians to block any significant measures that will rectify our current environmental situation? That's the white man trying to destroy Mother Earth for us brothers. First they took our freedom, now they're trying to take our planet!"

I shook my head and sighed.

"Okay Weston, first of all, that's a stretch even for you. And second...you're White."

"Here we go again with that. Cory, my brother, I told you, I did one of those mail-in test for genealogy. I'm like six eighty-sevenths African."

"Six eighty-sevenths?"

"Basically, if you go back about two dozen centuries, then my peoples and your peoples were the same peoples."

"Two dozen centuries? You know that's over two thousand years ago?"

"Right. I'm saying. And humans have been around for almost ten thousand years."

"Over two hundred thousand, actually."

"Even better. So with just two thousand years between you and me...we're practically brothers."

"I wouldn't say that. But, I've got work to do, so..."

"It's cool, do your thing. I'm just chilling. What do have going on today?"

"Prep for a client call." a voice called out.

Both of us looked over at the door to see my white knight- well, my black knight, really. Weston nodded as he left my office, addressing the authoritative woman in the entryway politely.

"Good morning, Ms. Vincent."

"Good morning, Weston."

Sofala closed the door behind him, and took a seat. We looked at each for a moment, then broke into a fit of mild laughter. She was the only reason I didn't completely loathe coming into work. Sofala was contagiously positive and energetic. She was the kind of person who valued opportunities for collaboration, and avoided the trappings of the agency gossip, and corporate apathy. She radiated that rare combination of approachable confidence, and genuine humility that never crossed into self-deprecation.

We met ages ago, back when I had just joined the company. Over the years, we had developed a strong friendship with a younger brother-older sister dynamic. She was my window to the socially treacherous world of colleague interaction. Whenever there was an afterwork event, midday break for coffee, or just a chance for the staff to get outside for a bit, someone would dash around the office to say something like:

"Lunch trucks are out, who wants to grab a bite?"

And I would try to quietly decline, but then Sofala would swoop in, usually with a casual question that was impossible for my awkwardness to decline.

"Hey Cory, want to grab lunch now with the tech guys, or wait a few minutes, and go with me and my team?"

"I guess, I'll go with you?" I'd respond.

"Great! See you in a bit!"

My appreciation of Sofala was based entirely in platonic, professional admiration. I was probably a little envious of her outgoing nature, especially since unless you counted Weston's "six eighty-sevenths" African ancestry, we were the only two people of color in the entire firm- not just in the main office, but counting the suburban branches as well.

I liked to say that we were the "flies in the marketing milk." Sofala preferred the expression "chocolates on the PR pillow." That right there summed up the differentiation between our two personalities far more accurately than any Myers-Briggs test results.

When she accepted a position with the West Coast office, the panic from hearing the news made me skip lunch for the next three days. I was thrilled that the otherwise monochromatic firm was promoting her to a leadership role, but also worried that tone deaf folks in the office (i.e., pretty much every one else in the office) would see me as the new involuntary ambassador for all things not-white.

After she left, the stress continued, remaining an underlying foundation of anxiety. So when the partners announced Sofala's return, I was so happy, I almost screamed right there in the conference room.

"It's good to see you again, Cory. Looks like you're doing pretty well. Everything been all right?"

"Aside from Weston, you know how it is. But otherwise, I can't complain."

"Well, you could, but who's going to listen, right?"

"How was the West Coast?"

"Warm. Expensive. Not as progressive as you might think. I mean, they talk the talk, but man, out there, almost nobody walks the walk."

"Sounds about right."

"I'll tell you though," Sofala walked past meand stared out the window, "the weather out there was on point. Forecast for today? Seventy-three degrees. But here? We've got…all of this."

"Yeah, but that's Minnesota, right. It's like—"

"What the hell was that!!!" Sofala jumped back.

"What?" I replied nervously.

"I saw something there. Through the clouds. Behind the buildings across the river!"

I dashed over and stared outside at the impenetrable grey veil of clouds obscuring the view. The panic in her voice made my pulse accelerate.

"I don't see anything." I said, regaining composure.

"There!" Sofala exclaimed, pointing so hard and quickly, that she chipped a nail on the glass. I was so startled by her outburst, that I bumped my head against the window again. I'd never seen her so agitated.

Rubbing my forehead, I looked to where she was pointing and saw why she had been so upset. In that moment, I was happy that I skipped breakfast, because my stomach clenched so tight, throwing up would've been as painful as it would've been inevitable.

My mind scrambled to come up with a rational excuse, but came up short. It was the same shockingly gargantuan, vaguely humanoid shape I thought that I'd imagined seeing earlier. There was no question as to whether this was just a delusion brought on by lack of sleep and too many soy lattes. It was real. It was huge. And most unnerving of all, it was steadily moving towards us.

"What the hell..." Sofala exhaled.

"This is unreal..." I stammered.

We both stared wide-eyed as the massive shape kept coming. I couldn't believe what we were witnessing any more than I could stop the involuntary tears of bewildered horror from spilling over my cheeks. The shape plowed through the rows of condominiums, sending concrete, glass and bodies plummeting.

"My god..." Sofala stammered.

The shape trudged through the final row of high-rise condos, and entered the river, sending massive waves crashing against the muddy banks. Behind it, thick plumes of gas and despair bellowed up from the ruins of the overpriced luxury housing it had just decimated. Within seconds, at least four hundred lives irrevocably wiped out.

The smoke unfurled carelessly, carrying the souls of hundreds killed in the devastation upwards until they blended seamlessly with the low-hanging clouds.

The safety glass of my office window was soundproof, but Sofala and I could feel the vibrations of the wanton destruction just across the river. The office was completely silent save for the sound of our labored breathing and the accelerated thumping of our hearts, which thankfully, hadn't stopped out of shock.

In response to unexplainable stimulus, the human body has numerous biological responses. Some people experience temporary paralysis. Others are charged with adrenaline, and an inherent desire to escape the situation. Luckily for me, Sofala wasn't one to freeze.

Sofala grabbed my arm and pulled us out of the office, just as another immense humanoid shape brushed against the side of the building, completely demolishing the northeastern corner where we'd just been standing.

The floor beneath us buckled as I consciously forced my feet to keep running. Left foot, right foot, left foot, right foot, just keep moving. Sofala was just a few inches ahead, and I could see the chaos over her shoulder as we ran.

Any other time, this is an impressive office space. We have the entire floor to ourselves and a completely open layout, but now running for our lives, through an obstacle course of copiers, meeting tables, and bean bag chairs, as our colleagues on all sides were screaming and pointing, running and diving for cover, I wished we'd been in a smaller workspace.

We made it to the doors leading to the central hallway,. I noticed Weston staring the gaping hole that used to be the sunny side of the office. Couldn't tell if he was frozen with fear, or genuinely that daft, that he didn't realize the treacherous gravity of the current situation.

"Weston!" Sofala yelled.

A massive tendril slithered in through the hole in the side of the building. The appendage was muscular and thick, glistening and wet from the April snow. It moved deliberately, wrapping around Weston's waist with astonishing precision and speed.

Sofala and I and the rest of the staff that hadn't made it out through the crowded, central hallway doors, stared in horror as the little mounds began to pulsate.

The mounds elongated, crawling across Weston's pale blue shirt in an oscillating motion. Smaller tentacles reached his hairline and flattened against his ears and face, encasing his head within a grotesque cocoon.

"What the hell…" I gasped.

As the last word stumbled past my lips, The cocoon abruptly withdrew, sloughing off the skin and hair of Weston's head in one fluid motion.

The larger main tendril around his waist constricted so violently that a large portion of his lower digestive organs, and the various fluids and substances contained within, were expelled ferociously through both his upper and lower orifices. The sound of the instantaneous excretion was worse than the visuals.

Before I had a chance to fully grasp the horror we'd just witnessed, the tendril yanked Weston's body violently towards the jagged opening of the building. His fleshless head, banged sickeningly against the exposed rebar of the craggy edges of the hole, catching briefly on the battered, exposed metal edge of the thick electrical conduit jutting out from the remains of the ceiling. He hung there for a few seconds, lodged in a grisly impasse.

His khakis were stained dark with bile and blood. They hung low on his hips, weighed down by the unnervingly biological bounty of internal organs floating, excrement and digestive fluids. The glossy, greyish-purple of his small intestines peaked out from his pant cuffs.

The tendril constricted and yanked again, causing the piping to shred his scalp, sending his skull cap flipping back.

Seeing his intracranial space exposed was so alarmingly abrupt and disturbing, it was almost comically surreal. The sensation was so overwhelming that I couldn't feel anything at all. My mind shut down, as his mangled body was dragged out into the cold, April air.

Weston's nightmarish death triggered a rush of adrenaline that increased Sofala's already intensely agitated state. She looked at me. I couldn't see her looking at me, but I could feel her gaze. I was frozen, staring unblinkingly at the irregular stains that served as the last remnants of our hideously deceased, colleague.

I never liked Weston. Nobody in the office really did. But Weston wasn't a bad person. He was merely annoying. Everyone is, has been, or eventually will be considered annoying to someone else. But that's not enough to warrant disembowelment and scalping via ginormous extraterrestrial monster. Even at his worst, there was nothing he'd ever done to earn such a horrendous fate.

Sofala grabbed me. Her grip on my arm freed me from my temporary paralysis. I looked at her. What transpired was completely wordless, and completely understood. The look conveyed more than lunchtime chats, texts, or emails ever could. I nodded in agreement.

We had to escape.

DOWNTOWN

We turned and ran, dodging falling lights and ceiling tiles. We ignored injured and overwhelmed coworkers as we hurdled over toppled furniture. This wasn't a matter of callous indifference. This was a matter of survival.

"If we could make it to the fire escape, there might have a chance." Sofala gasped, "They're in the center of the building, hopefully the damage hasn't reached them."

We pushed through our crying, screaming, and rapidly vanishing colleagues, as dozens of massive, tendrils burst through the openings, grabbing their victims, and pulling off their faces, before yanking the casually dressed, overpaid professionals out of the building.

Coughing through the polluted air that was saturated with dust, sweat, blood, and drywall, we carved a path through the growing piles of twisted bodies, we held our arms up to protect our heads.

Finally, we reached the fire escape. The building shuddered violently as Sofala and I descended. Several people toppled over the guardrails, plummeting through the darkness, noisily banging heads and limbs against lower stairs and guardrails. Every single one of them screamed all the way down, until the dull impact silenced their cries.

We'd reached the ground level and climbed over the fallen. Their bodies were merely an obstacle. Just pieces of people we had to get over and past to freedom.

Sofala pushed through the doors. Light from the outside flooded the in, illuminating a catastrophic level of major metropolitan devastation. Along with several hundred escapees, we tore out of the building. Pausing to catch my breath, I looked up in astonishment.

We had traded the terrors inside the office, for an unfathomable nightmare unfurling on the sidewalks. It wasn't that we'd left the frying pan, to jump into fire. We'd escaped the stove top fire, only to land face-first into the raging flames of hell.

"Watch out!" Sofala yelled, tackling me to the ground. A five-foot square chunk of steel and concrete exploded on the sidewalk inches away from where I'd been standing.

"Thank you!" I exclaimed.

"We've got to keep moving!" Sofala retorted.

The already dark sky was furthered obscured by the calamity of an unrelenting onslaught as boulder-sized knots of metal and plastic rained down on the street. An avalanche of bodies, plunged onto the asphalt crushing cars, trucks, and pedestrians with a remorseless finality.

The street lamps and traffic that hadn't been demolished, stood bent at odd angles, patiently awaiting their inevitable demise, beneath the steel support beams and decorative stonework of downtown Minneapolis.

The sky was literally falling, but the intersections were flooded with waves of heat stoked by the fires that seemed to obscure every window in the remnants of the building along the avenues and boulevards. Debris clouds of smoke shrouded every space not currently being occupied by the thousands who lived and worked in the warehouse district.

Looming above the frenzied mayhem of were the gargantuan figures. Dozens of them tore through the downtown Minneapolis. They trudged casually, flattening block after block of loft buildings, fancy restaurants, big retailers, and small storefront boutiques with an almost apathetic ease. Theaters, galleries, public art installations, government buildings, and banking centers that had withstood the unflinching cruelty of history were reduced to misshapen piles of flaming rubble.

The skyline that was a visual symphony of architectural design and urban engineering was reduced to ruins in less than an hour. The noise was deafening. Between the security alarms, emergency broadcast signals, and anguished screams of the dying, it was hard to hear your own thoughts.

The giant creatures vanished as quickly as they'd appeared. The clouds drifted north. The rain and snow dissipated. The stark contrast between the serene view above, and the vibrantly intense colors, smells, and sounds of the tragedy below, was obscenely disconcerting.

Sofala and I found refuge near the ruins of the stadium. We stood in silence, connected to each other, and the handful of others who had made it to the safety of The Commons, the large open park whose grass quietly suffocated under a thick layer of dust.

Questions of what had happened and hung heavily over a sea of exhausted, sweat covered faces, that stared out over the scattered piles of corpses. There were ad executives, bankers, uniformed delivery men, retired silver foxes, grad students, bartenders, police officers, homeless men, women and children of every gender, race, and size lined the streets in a ghastly display of posthumous equality.

LOOK!" a voice in the crowd yelled.

Numerous hands began pointing frantically at the sky. The sunlight faded to shadow, and the blue canopy of the downtown sky was eclipsed by an ominous mass as thousands of giant, vaguely humanoid silhouettes filled our entire field of vision. Witnessing the impending ruination above our heads, the realization hit me.

What we'd survived this morning was an appetizer. We had survived the first wave. Whatever those things were, they had destroyed downtown and the northeast neighborhoods of the city with an almost laughable ease.

Sofala grabbed my hand. I felt the same sense of same horror pulsing through her palms.

Her cellphone rang. She wiped her eyes and let go of my hand. I wiped my own eyes, and dusted off a few layers of dirt and debris that had collected on my shirt and slacks. I sat down in the grass a few steps away, so she could have a little bit of privacy while she took the call and looked around at the other people gathered around.

I was surprised, not in the amount of variation between body types, skin tones, hairstyles, and other indicators proving that contrary to what many believe about the biggest city in Minnesota, there actually is a wealth of diversity among the residents. No, I was surprised by the lack of interaction.

When you see news coverage of any major disaster, there are always scenes of people banding together to weather the literal and/or figurative storms. The cynic in me used to assume it was the producers who constructed the pieces. It was the broadcast precursor to those 'restore your faith in humanity' listicles you'd see pop up on social media.

But part of me hoped it was true. That when the chips were all the way down, people would see the bigger picture and just finally, for a brief moment, be decent to each other.

That was not the case here.. Nobody cared about anyone they didn't know. They weren't reaching out to each other, or comforting the lost and crying. The few people gathered here were just happy to be alive.

"That was Angelique!" Sofala yanked me to my feet.

"Who's Angelique?" I asked.

"Daughter of a friend. She's been staying with me since I got back to Minneapolis. She said the damage hasn't reached the south side yet. A friend is meeting her there, and he might have a way out. If we can make it to the Mall of America, we can get out of town with them."

"Okay then, let's go to the mall."

WEST BANK

The entrance to the garage was completely impenetrable, but Sofala and I were able to find an abandoned sedan that still had the keys in the ignition. As we headed south through the apocalyptic landscape that used to be some of the most desirable commercial property in the state, I chuckled to myself, thinking how strangely funny it was that of all the places that could serve as the rendezvous for our point of rescue, we were going to the Mall of America.

Even though it'd been a few months since I'd last been there, MOA is hands down my absolute favorite place in the Twin Cities- possibly even the state. Not only is the huge mall damned near impossible to get lost in, thanks to the floor plan (it's basically a giant ring), there are hundreds of stores, restaurants, and other attractions offering anything you could possibly be looking for.

Some locals claim that they don't like to shop there, or even visit, unless they're hosting out of town guests. It's no different than when a teenaged poser pretends to be disinterested. Remember how back in the day, posers would love a rapper or band, until that rapper or band played on a late night show, then they'd scoff and say that the rapper or band "sold out," as if the rapper or band wasn't trying to make a living from their art? It was like that.

On the other hand, some locals claim to not dig MOA because it was built was built on the site of the old Met Stadium, and because the mall is too big and they have trouble finding parking, and they don't like the building design, or how crowded it can get.

The real reason though, why so many locals claim to not dig it, is because MOA shoppers and employees come from every walk of life. Rich or poor, POCI or White, old or young, as long as you're not causing any trouble, nobody cares MOA welcomes everyone. You can't say that about anywhere else in the NorthStar State.

Lots of people here like to pretend that they're inclusive, progressive, and tolerant, but the proof is in the pudding. If all of your friends, family, romantic partners, colleagues, and neighbors are the same color, that's not happenstance, that's telling. If you don't have any close friends of a different gender or sexual preference, that's not happenstance, that's telling. When you save up thousands of dollars (or lean on your parents) so you can travel to the other side of the world to volunteer so you can help the kids, but are afraid to set foot in North Minneapolis, that's telling.

I thought of all of this as we slowly made our way, and found myself growing angry. Well, maybe not angry per se, but annoyed. Maybe after this catastrophe, we'll finally figure it out. I wouldn't bet on it, but maybe.

We'd made it out of downtown, around the bending overpass that ran above the highway, where Washington Avenue turns into Cedar Avenue. Compared to the horrors of downtown and Northeast part of the city, the West Bank neighborhood was relatively unscathed. Traffic was practically bumper to bumper, a mix of both people trying to escape the carnage, those who had pulled over to star in terrified amazement at the damage, and a small number of those who used the catastrophe as an excuse to abandon any notions of civility they may have held.

Now, freed from the threat of consequences, these same types of people were terrorizing the good residents of the West Bank. Windows were broken, stores looted, fires of varying sizes and origin dotted the neighborhood landscape like crumbs on a carpet. Those big ass aliens didn't have to smash through a neighborhood to destroy it. We could do well enough on our own.

We inched along slowly, progressing with caution, avoiding the shouting revelers and shrieking victims as best as possible, until we reached the intersection where Cedar crosses Riverside Avenue. Traffic grinded to a complete standstill in front of the havoc that was unfolding in the streets. It wasn't a riot. Riots have purpose. This was agitated mayhem for agitated mayhem's sake.

"We should probably get out and walk from here."
Sofala resigned.

"Good idea," I quipped.

We got out of the car, and trudged along the crowded sidewalks. The West Bank neighborhood was always lively. The mix of Somali, LatinX, old hippies, young service workers, medical residents, and University grad students made for an eclectic symphony of sights and sounds. No matter who you were or where you were from, all eyes were either staring at the otherworldly threat descending upon us, even those causing trouble occasionally glanced up.

At various intervals along the sidewalk, they were dead and broken bodies lying in contorted poses, intermixed with security tags torn from ill-gotten wares recently liberated from the storefronts. The damage was almost entirely perpetuated by young white men in their late teens and early twenties, but the few security and law enforcement officers that were able to maneuver between the swirling masses were more focused on chasing and detaining the beige, brown, and black faces defending their livelihoods.

Sofala and I walked carefully, moving with the flow of the crowds, desperately maintaining as inconspicuous a profile as possible. It was impossible to tell the difference between the man-made atrocities currently in progress, and the otherworldly disaster from which we'd escaped.

The thought of being seriously injured, or even killed, by some random group of kids stealing cases of beer, when we had just narrowly avoided being annihilated by a group of giant aliens was so bizarrely ironic, it made me laugh. We turned and went deeper into the neighborhood to find a less congested, and less hazardous, route.

Ahead of us, we saw an older woman carrying groceries. A couple of blonde-haired boys jumped out from behind a car and tackled her. The impact of her head smacking pavement was loud enough that we heard it, from a little less than half a block away.

The blonde heads, who were still laughing and taunting the poor old woman, as she struggled to get to her feet and collect her groceries, noticed us. The taller of the two spat and frowned. I couldn't tell if he was frowning out of anger, because we were disrupting their fun, or if he was just confused by our appearance. Taking advantage of our inadvertent diversion, the old woman grabbed as many groceries as she could, and scuttled off down the street.

"Looks like you've got the wrong street!" he yelled.

"Looks like you've got the wrong...face!" I yelled back.

That caught him off guard. I've never been good with trash talk or witty comebacks. He looked at me and frowned again, this time with an obnoxious smirk smeared across his peach fuzz-covered chin.

He put two fingers in his mouth and whistled. Blonde heads began appearing from behind cars. Young blonde men in red jackets began coming out of the homes they'd been burglarizing. I was completely surrounded.

"Let me go!" Sofala yelled.

I whipped around to see three Blonde heads, dragging her out from her behind the low-rise apartment building. They were yanking on her arms and taunting her. My revulsion at her treatment was immediate and visceral.

Blinded by anger, I lunged towards them screaming. I was so incensed and hyper-focused on freeing Sofala from the grinning, groping hands of the Blonde heads surrounding her, I didn't notice another Blonde head running out of a yard, coming straight at me. I didn't see his fist until it crashed into my forehead. I felt my back hit the cold pavement. My vision of the outside world shattered into vignettes as I faded in and out of consciousness. The shoulders of the lead Blonde head shaking as he laughed. But then, he stopped laughing.

Through my aching, hazy vision, I saw a massive group of coming around the corner. Teenage Somali boys lead a battalion of tattoo-covered bicyclists, middle aged vegans, Black queer artists, First Nations activists, canvas-clad gutter punks, smokers, dealers, undergrads and weirdos. The West Bank was coming to our rescue.

The blonde heads did the math in their heads, and scattered off into the neighborhood. Two comely Hmong girls sporting asymmetrical haircuts and faded university sweaters helped me to my feet, while a guy with a red goatee and shiny white bald head rushed over with a couple of the Somali boys and tended to Sofala.

"Thank you!" I squeaked out, rubbing my head.

"Of course." said one of the Hmong girls, "Those guys have been wreaking havoc all morning."

I ran to Sofala and gave her a hug.

"Oh no!" a man who was old enough to remember the early sixties vividly yelled, "They're coming back!"

I thought he was referring to the blonde heads, but my stomach dropped when I saw him pointing up. It was the second wave of big ass aliens. The ones who had darkened the sky as Sofala and I escaped downtown. Thousands of them obscured the view, just a few hundred feet above our heads. They weren't closing in on us. They were here.

"There were only a dozen that hit downtown," Sofala exclaimed, "there's got to be at least a hundred thousands of those things now!"

I started to feel dizzy. Damn, that blonde head must've hit me harder than I thought. The last thing I remember before passing out was Sofala reaching towards me. Her lips were moving but I couldn't understand her words.

DREAM

"What are you going to do besides get mad?"

It's 1991. Chicago. Unseasonably warm for being so close to the end of Fall. My stomach hurts. I'm on the ground. I can feel the cold of the cement through the butt of my jeans. I just got my ass kicked again.

A shadow fell over me, as I sat on the side walk holding my midsection, trying to stop the pain. Shadow moves again. It's Mr. Backstrom. I can smell the heat of his breath as he leans in close to me. His dark skin is permanently creased into deep folds around his prematurely aged eyes. He licks his dry lips and spreads his mouth into a sympathetic sideways smile. He offers his hand. I take it.

Backstrom is relatively new in the neighborhood, but he'd quickly made a name for himself hosting holiday parties at the rec center, and making sizable donations at church. They weren't crazy big, but they were big enough that he gets his name listed in the program almost Sunday. He seemed like any other grownup who had a little money, and had taken an altruistic interests in our community.

I'd never really seen him this close before. He was much older than I was, but there's a mischievous quiet behind his eyes. A spark of mystery hinting at a life filled with lessons learned the hard way.

"Thanks, Mr. Backstrom."

"Don't thank me. Answer the question."

"What question?"

"The question that Jefferson boy yelled just before he kicked your ass. The question I just asked you right now, helping you up. What are you going to do besides get mad?"

"I don't know. Nothing I can do about it." I sputter, swatting at the dirt on my jeans. It was true. There wasn't much I could do about it. Jerry Jefferson was bigger, faster, and stronger than I would ever be.

"You think that because you're not as big as he is, that means you deserve to get beat around like that?"

"Well, no?"

"Okay then. And you know that he's not going to stop just because you wish he would."

"Yeah, I guess."

"That means that you're going to have to do something to make him stop."

"What am I supposed to do?" I'm angry now, "You think I like this? If I knew what to do, I'd do it."

"You sure about that?"

"Mr. Backstrom, with all respect, if you're about to share some dumb cliché about standing up to bullies, save it. That doesn't make them go away. It just makes them come after you even harder."

"No you're right," Backstrom puffs on his cigarette.

"I'm right?"

"Yeah, you're right. Standing up to him isn't enough. You've got to end this. You've got to do something to make him stop."

"Like what?"

Mr. Backstrom stares at me hard. I'd never seen an expression like that before. It was like he was trying to size me up, but scare me away at the same time, like an office manager at the end of a bad interview.

"How old are you?" He asks, riffling around in his jacket.

 "Eleven."

"Eleven? Old enough. Take this." he holds out his hand.

Instinctively, I reach for it. He drops something small and heavy into my young palms. I open my hands and stared at the impromptu gift.

I recognize it from music class. It's a capo, a tiny device that you strapped around the neck of your guitar to change the pitch of the strings. It lets you play in different keys but use the same fingerings for chords. This is an older version. It's a small, flat metal bar, with little notches in the sides. The bar is coated in rubber, with a nylon strap connected to one end. On the other end of the strap, is a flat plastic tab, with two little posts sticking out of it..

"A capo? What, you want me to sing him a song?"

"Watch it," Backstrom snaps, "Mind your tone."

"Sorry, Mr. Backstrom."

"Okay then." Mr. Backstrom flicks his cigarette, "What you want to do is wrap this around your fingers, and when you punch him, aim for the space right between his upper lip and the bottom of his nose."

"But I've tried hitting him before."

"Not like this you haven't." Backstrom smirks, "You pop him good right there, with the metal side of the capo across your knuckles, it's a messy thing. Lots of blood vessels in the upper lip see. You hit him good, you're going to pop those vessels, going to look and feel a lot worse that it is. While he's distracted by all the blood and pain, he'll be confused. That's when you grab him, with both arms, right above the knees and push. Should make him fall flat on his back, and knock the wind out of him."

"I don't know if I can do all that." I say wide-eyed. I'd never heard an adult openly advocate violence so blatantly.

"Well," Backstrom lights another cigarette, "You'd better figure something out, because Here he comes."

I look down the block. Sure enough, Jerry was heading back towards us. I hurriedly wrap the capo around my fingers, with the metal bar sitting flat across my knuckles. My heart is racing. I'm trying to remember Backstrom said.

"Hey punk! I thought I told you to---"

Before he can finish his sentence, I explode. My sloppy jab catches him squarely in the soft part of his face just above his upper lip, below the bottom of his nose. The blood spurt upon impact catches us both by surprise. Jerry screams, grabbing at his face.

"Take him down. Above the knees!" Backstrom calls.

The impact of the tackle sends Jerry sprawling across the pavement. His back makes an stomach churning sound as it ricochets off the sidewalk. I climb off of him and feel ill.

Neither of my parents had ever struck me in anger. I remember spankings as a kid, but that stopped around middle school. Violence made me nauseous. Physical altercation was too primal, too brutal, too uncivilized.

I look down at Jerry. He's still conscious. His face breaks out in bright purple bruises. Scars are already beginning to form, sullying the otherwise flawless, dark beige complexion of his skin. His bloody moustache stains his shirt, and drips onto the sidewalk. Tears in his eyes are more from confusion and fear, than anger or pain. The sick feeling in my stomach fades. Replaced by a darker sensation.

He deserves this. He'd tormented me for years. I want him to feel what I'd felt all those times he humiliated me and beat on me. I want him to suffer the same way I did. Then I realize something even more disturbing. I didn't just want him hurt. I want him dead.

"That's what you get!" I cry, kicking Jerry in the gut.

"No," Backstrom grabs my shoulder, "he's already been beaten. The message has been delivered. Anything more, and the message becomes motivation."

"But?" I'm confused now, "You're the one who told me how to beat him."

"A man crosses you, you've got to respond in a way that he won't want to cross you again. You have to put fear in his heart and his mind. The kind of fear that's reflexive. You see that look in his eyes right now?" he points at Jerry who has morphed into a smaller version of the big ass aliens that will destroy my adopted hometown over two decades from now, "He knows that if he ever messes with you again, it's his ass. But if you keep taking those cheap little pot-shots at him, keep kicking him when he's down? That fear will get pushed out and replaced with humiliation. And there's nothing more motivating than humiliation. It's a dangerously powerful recipe for revenge. Get it?"

"I understand."

The sky falls black. The Jerry/Alien melts into the ground. Backstrom takes a long drag of his cigarette, and when he goes to ash the tip, he vanishes. I'm alone in the dark with blood on my knuckles.

Something is coming, but I can't run.

BIG ASS ALIENS CONTINUES IN BOOK 2:

SOUTHSIDE PRIDE

ABOUT THE AUTHOR

T. Aaron Cisco is a contemporary Afrofuturist, musician, and award-winning television producer. He is also a contributing writer for TwinCitiesGeek.com, with a focus on TV, Race & Culture. His other works include Teleportality, Dragon Variation, The Preternaturalist, and Shadow of the Valley.